Charles Augustus Keeler

The Promise of the Ages

Charles Augustus Keeler

The Promise of the Ages

ISBN/EAN: 9783741187582

Manufactured in Europe, USA, Canada, Australia, Japa

Cover: Foto ©Andreas Hilbeck / pixelio.de

Manufactured and distributed by brebook publishing software
(www.brebook.com)

Charles Augustus Keeler

The Promise of the Ages

THE PROMISE OF THE AGES

BY

CHARLES AUGUSTUS KEELER

Yet I doubt not thro' the ages one increasing purpose runs,
And the thoughts of men are widen'd with the process of the suns.
—TENNYSON.

To Joseph Le Conte

Seeker, whose science o'ermasters the spirit's despair,—
Teacher, whose truth mounts to heaven in worship and
  prayer,—
Prophet, whose deeds are a witness of faith, free and
  strong,—
Not to tender vain tribute to thee, do I pledge thee my
  song,
But to gain, from thy life and thy love, benediction, dear
  friend,
To hallow my labor with graces thy presence can lend.

INTRODUCTION.

The law of evolution forms the keynote of this
latter nineteenth century. It is the principle of trans-
formation, of growth, of progress. It has profoundly
modified our thought in all fields of observation and
speculation, reconstructing the foundations of science,
and challenging the dogmas of religion. In striking
contrast to this modern conception of the origin of the
forms of existence, is the more venerable doctrine of
a divine creation, executed consciously by the volition
of God in order that His love might find expression in
tangible form. The clash of these two opinions, with
their innumerable side issues, is termed the conflict
of science and religion. If religion is to prevail in this
conflict, it will be at the price of certain concessions
popularly deemed of intrinsic importance, and espe-
cially by the surrender of all which cannot be defended
by reason, namely, the miraculous.

Upon this basis, I have attempted, in the following
pages, to present the struggles of an earnest mind with
some of the modern life-problems; and, in the per-

sonality of the Prophet, to exhibit these questions as they pass through the mind of the idealist.

The poem recognizes the principle of evolution, but seeks to transcend this with the higher thought of the ultimate reality of the spirit. It is an attempt at a synthesis of the essential ideas of Darwin and Emerson. The frank use of the subject-matter of science in poetry may be called in question, but a justification for this is found in the recognition of love as the animating principle beneath all the conflict and tumult of the ages.   C. A. K.

BERKELEY CAL.
August, 1896

THE PROMISE OF THE AGES.

THE PROMISE OF THE AGES.

BOOK I.

In meadows prank'd with sun-enamour'd flowers,
'Mid cool wood wilds, fern-paved and leaf-embower'd,
On mountain steeps, by ocean's storm-rent strand,
Young Percival, unwearied, wandered on
Through life's fair pageant, truth intoxicate,—
Vain searcher—pleading at the van of time
For some still voice from earth's mute lips of stone,
Some sign amid the senseless trees that sway—
Canst find no respite from inconstancy?
The very seasons glided 'neath his gaze
Like ebb and flow of ocean's tireless tide,
And fair day floated far on wings of gloom.
The birds, o'erladen with their golden song,
Swept like a gale of joy through spring's glad bow'rs,
By faith impelled to love's blest miracle.
Then busy bills upgather'd flexile sprays,

9

The willow's bloom or drifted thistle-down,—
And homes were shaped to hold the dappled eggs.
Life's mystery revealed the callow young,
By watchful care upreared, by love made strong;
But, like the leaves that fall from autumn's boughs,
They scatter'd from the groves and left them drear.
"O Time, with thrifty fingers weaving all
This mighty garb of earth," cried Percival,
"Canst thou not show me truth's enduring form
Lurking within this guise of changefulness?"
But time swept on and rested not to tell,
While doubt and gloom encompassed Percival.
"O what is truth, where all is death or change,
And what is love in life's inconstancy,
And what is life but shadow doomed to fade:
Truth, love, life, all a mockery and show!"
Thus, bosomed in his own despairing dream,
He saw life's shadow-splendor melt away
To emptiness and death. O heart forlorn,
Arise from bitterness and seek anew!
Thou hast not delved in man's unfathomed heart
For treasure earth denies thee! Solitude
Can never yield thy guerdon, vainly craved!
For, ever, ere hope's darkest hour is spent,
Come peace and joy to lift the heart that pines;
No spirit lives but some loved counterpart

Awaits the day to greet its kindred soul.
So Percival, when hope and trust had fled,
Found, in a life that brooded o'er his own,
The matchless rapture of a loving mind.
A man of mighty destiny was he,
Whom time had treasured to the uttermost.
His fragile form the weary years had bent,
While silverly his locks fell round his brow,
And, in the fire of eyes deep sunk from age,
A light gleamed forth that pierced the veil of tears.
To Percival he seemed as one divine,
So large his nature, so serene his mind,
His thought, transfigured from the dross of earth,
In heaven's more ample regions roving free.
A prophet, Percival proclaimed his friend,
And would not hear him called by other name.
Large-hearted creature, he revealed himself,—
A messenger with life's good word to bear
To all, from that exhaustless mind of love.
They wandered oft in fond companionship,
'Mid silvan haunts where roved the shy wood-things,
Through forest halls, by wild birds tenanted,
That rang with notes so sweet and far away,
It seemed the singing choir of heav'n was heard;
And here in nature's temple worshiped they,
The wind's soft organ tones low antheming,

11

The brook's pure waters praying ceaselessly,
And all the air attuned to peace and joy.
One eve they lingered past the set of sun,
The golden glow slow waning in the west,
While silent stars, long pent in day's bright glare,
Came stealing forth to watch the somber night,
And deep'ning shadows spread across the plain.
Then looked they starward through the boundless
    deep,
Awed by the solemn miracle of night,
When Percival gan ask the cause of all,—
The genesis and growth of stars and worlds,
The uncreated, shaped and bodied forth
By law's resistless process, time ordained.
Then answered him the Prophet, thought imbued,
As one inspired by God's transcendent toil,
Thus speaking in the earnest hush of night:

"In the beginning was God, who was wholly a Spirit
    of love,—
A Spirit of limitless love, with His measureless treas-
    ure to give,—
With His infinite beauty of love, to be given sublimely
    away.
And the Spirit of God was awake in the darkness that
    brooded afar,

Awake in the night and the void, with the slumberless
    love at His heart;
And out of His loving there streamed, through the
    night and the void supreme,
A numberless throng of His children, to share with
    his infinite good.
They thronged through the darkness in silence, un-
    knowing how fair they were formed,
Unknowing the wealth and the wonder of beauty they
    bore through the night;
God only aware of the wonder His will had achieved
    of His love,
Aware of the beauty of man, that was shrouded in
    mist of the stars.
Through man grew the glory of heaven,—the splen-
    dors of earth and of air,
And the tumult and trouble of time, as it speeds on
    its weariless way;
For man is the image of God—the wonderful work
    of His thought—
And the world is the image of man —of his measure-
    less, mystical mind,
Of his mind that is growing to freedom, through æons
    of turbulent time,—
From chaos upgrowing to knowledge, from envy
    expanding to love.

From star-dust to Godhood still climbing, man meas-
    ures the fathomless spheres,—
With love and with tears he is sounding their ultimate
    deeps,—
And this is the way of his climbing, to look in the face
    of his God:

When man first breathed of the breath which his
    bountiful Father had given,
When first His thought went forth, to make him a
    world for a home,
There was nothing but law in His world that had
    triumphed o'er chaos and night,
The alterless law of His being, unswerving through
    cycles of change;
And out of His law and His thought grew the palpitant
    star-dust of heaven,
The quivering star-dust, aglow with the fury of worlds
    in the making.
White-hot was the strenuous beating of infinite labor-
    ing atoms,—
The atoms that rolled into suns, with the rumble of
    turbulent thunder,—
That throbbed in the nebulous suns that were rushing
    through darkness supreme.
Each star took the station assigned it in heaven's
    unsearchable span,

14

And sang as it swept in its orbit that turned at the
    lodestar's control;
For thus was ordained by the Father, that harmony
    ever should rule;
And thus sang the spheres, in their motion, of har-
    mony perfect through time.

From the vaporous stars' mighty girdles, the planets
    were scattered afar,
Foredoomed to a path through the heavens enchained
    to the orb they had spurned.
The sun, in a quivering phrenzy, shook Neptune away
    from her side,
And shrank with a shuddering tremor away from her
    radiant child;
Uranus was born in a tumult of furious fiery flame,
And Saturn swept forth in his wonder, and Jupiter
    burst through the night,—
The mightiest child of the sun from his luminous
    parent was rent;
Then Mars, the presager of battles, and Earth, where
    the battles were fought,—
Fair Earth, the kind mother who fostered the faltering
    spirit of man,—
Fair Earth, blessed battle-ground, holy, where man
    struggled on to the light,—

15

Where still he is toiling for freedom, for beauty, for
truth, and for love.
While Earth, with her volatile splendor, was robing
the darkness in light,
Fair Venus was born in the heavens, a witness of
widening love;
And Mercury, loath to relinquish the sun that had
held him so long,
The last of the planets created, was hurled into space
without end.

Thus, slowly and solemnly builded, while time urged
its way through the void,
The stars and the planets, evolving, reflected the
beauty of mind,—
Reflected the order and purpose that God on His
sons had bestowed,—
Unfolding the power of heaven,—upholding, fulfilling
the law.
Stars, stars, multitudinous stars, that tremble afar
through the æther,
That baffle the mind with their number, wide-reaching
away through the gloom,—
Swift speeding, with planets attendant, in orbits unerringly true,
All molded of mists of the heavens, in the fiery forge
of the soul,—

THE PROMISE OF THE AGES.

Not all of thy wonders and numbers can equal the
    scope of a soul!

O man, with the earth thou art weaving, and fashion-
    ing all of thy soul,
How little thou dream'st that thy fabric is utterly
    wrought of the soul,—
How little thou knowest thy greatness for evil or good
    to the whole!
Yea, verily, God has endowed thee with power of
    perfect control,
And through thee the troubles of æons in infinite
    majesty roll!

The Prophet ceased, and hushed was ev'ry sound,
The earth outstretched beneath, the stars o'erhead,
The night attuned to deep solemnity.
Then walked they forth, no words escaping them,
For God's mysterious presence seemed so near,
As star by star trooped by in splendor dight,—
Worlds limitless in night's eternal breast.
The wind's low harp played tones æolean
Across the grassy glades, and lips were heard
By Percival that syllabled sweet strains —
Wind voices singing low their vesper lay:

THE PROMISE OF THE AGES.

Sibylline singing,
Rolling and ringing,
Weary of winging
Its musical way —
Pauses appealing,
Its meaning concealing,
Its rapture revealing
In heaven's array.

Starry forms dancing,
Gliding and glancing
Where mists are enhancing
Their mystical glee,
Pause in their pleasure,
And leap toward the measure
Of sibylline treasure,
So wanton and free.

BOOK II.

O moment big as destiny, that fills
A lifelong brooding with its fruitfulness !
O thought, transcending time and change and dread,
By hearts of love for aye interpreted !
In Percival's fond mind the Prophet's form,
Illumined dimly by the stars' cold glow,
Stood like a pillar of eternal stone
To thrill his sight with ceaseless wonderment;
And through the silence rang those earnest words
In haunting tones of solemn mystery: —
The stars — man's thought incarnate in the sky —
The earth—man's home, in love and wonder wrought—
And man—the Alpha and Omega, son
Of God Himself, who rules and loves His child !
What themes unthought were here to peer upon;
What weird brain fancies teemed in hill and sky,
All unrevealed to man's insensate ken !
This creature, shaped by time's unceasing toil,
To crown life's pageant with a fitting show,

The Master made a god, time fashioning,—
Building a universe of thought alone.
The neophyte knew not the Prophet's mind,
Veiled in its mystery of subtle lore,
And doubt oppressed him with a fresh dismay
When love, new-grown and strong, could scarce compel
Compliance to a creed of fancy wrought.
His young heart, panting with adorement meet,
Rebelled as earth's firm floor beneath him swayed,
And all tried things grew insecure and vain.
The Master felt his skeptic mood and said,
" Fear not the doubt that busies thee with pain,
And robs my words of aught of worth or pow'r;
'T is half of truth, and faith supplies the rest,
For Doubt and Faith, twin daughters of the soul,
With hands uplifted hold the cup of truth,
No guerdon granting to the parchèd brain,
Save when by each the suppliant stands approved.
Thus is this dream of earth and heav'n made real.
See at our feet this senseless form of stone,
Dead nothingness of time-ensculptured clay,
Wherewith the mind regenerates the past,
Pent in its passive form, and reads therein
A mighty fable of forgotten days—
The conflict of the ages—earth the field

And heaven the prize of battle, still unwon."
" And wilt thou tell me, Prophet, all the lore
Of storied legend writ upon the stone,
And wilt thou read the scriptures treasured there?"
So pleaded Percival, and thus replied
His teacher, thought engrossed in earth's grand theme:

" In deep-embosomed silentness the earth enfolds a
      tale,
With misery and mystery enwoven page on page;
With misery and victory triumphantly proclaimed,—
Triumphant tribulation for the garnishment of time!
I gaze upon the story in the writing on the rocks,
The story of the ages since the birth of Mother Earth,
And O my heart is brimming with the beauty of the tale,
And O my senses falter at its magnitude and might!

Old ocean, ever laboring upon the shores of time,
With pitiless persistency engulfing rock and strand;
Ye rivers, ever rushing from the mountains to the sea,
With freight of sand to bear away, to build the ocean's
      floor;
Ye pelting rains, that patter on the parapets of earth—
I marvel at the story ye have stored beneath the deep,—
The story of the cooling of the incandescent earth,--
The conquering of fire by the elements of air!

O who can thread the labyrinth of far-receding time,
And stand amid the wilderness on Earth's Archæan
    shore,
Where darkest desolation dims the dawning with its
    gloom,
And black the barren rocks are thrust above the
    seething sea,
To cling amidst the sullen clouds that veil the sordid
    land?

The sea was fiercely howling then on bleak tempes-
    tuous strand,
And fierce the thund'ring fires smote and shook the
    shattered shore,
But not an ear was there to hear, and not a heart to
    quail!
The rocks have locked the mystery of earth's re-
    motest time,
Amid their silent fastnesses securely stored away;
But O the prying hand of man, and O the prying
    brain!
With infinite preparings, in the darkness of the deep,
Another age was dawning with the mystery of life,
With the seeds of all eternity, the germs of all to be,
Lying lifeless in the ocean with its latent life sublime,—
Lying silent, with a patience God alone can under-
    stand,

With His watching and His waiting for the crowning
    form of man.
In the silent seas Silurian the frame of man was
    planned,
While feeble groping creatures swarmed amid the
    troubled deep,
And myriads of mollusks crowded all the crumbling
    shores,
Crowded all the shores that shuddered in the silent
    lapse of time.
And now the rocks are telling me their tale Devonian,
Of mighty fish in armor clad, that throng'd the
    throbbing tide,
All silent now in endless sleep of stony death sublime;
For fate has swept the sounding sea with carnage near
    and far,
And death was weeding all the waste in times
    Devonian.
The forests of the age of coal, I see in splendor dight,
With all their wild luxuriance of fern and tropic fen,
Of waving plumes and tangled trees, that bend above
    the bog,
And silent creatures growing into potency and might.
Now dawns the day of reptile hosts, uncouth and
    strange of form,
Uncanny things that swim and creep, and lift them-
    selves in air,—

Huge ichthyosaurs and dragons scaled, misshapen,
    vast in bulk,
Like monarchs of the nether world on destiny's fair
    shore.

Time wears away its wonderment as ages slowly roll,
The low succumb to higher types, the weary faint and
    die;
The age has come for nobler forms,—the reptile slinks
    away;
The peerless bird ascends the blue, the mammal
    treads the plain.
He tramples o'er the fallen host, he conquers all the
    land,
He rises in his majesty and proves the might of
    mind.
The dreary age of ice may come to test the work of
    time,
And whiten all the lovely land with deadly driving
    snow,
But still the southward-sweeping horde, unconquer-
    ably strong,
Is reaching ever higher with a craving unrepressed,—
Growing eagerly to manhood with its victory of soul,
With the limitless possessions that are placed within
    its reach.

Triumphantly the task of time looks backward o'er
    its span,
And sees the tender love of God, fruition find in
    man."

His words upon the silent air took wing,
The heedless wind their accents hurrying
Afar where thought their echo scarce could tell,
As, note by note, to nothingness they fell;
But Percival with busy brain had caught
Each syllable with earth's far pageant fraught,
And cherished all its wonder. Age by age
Had earth unrolled each mighty figured page,
Like some old Sibyl's pond'rous book of fate,
Where time had writ what death might consecrate.
And this was truth,—this faith revealed in stone,
In tablets graved ere Moses stood alone
Before his God, to learn what high decree
Should vest him with divine supremacy,—
This faith the dead past bore to life again,—
This growth, this striving, this enduring pain!
So Percival believed, and so he said;
The Prophet, musing, shook his hoary head:
" Thy mind too easily is set at rest;
Too soon wouldst thou conclude thy endless quest.
With tireless mind press on, nor rest content

Till thou hast gained the soul's far firmament.
With endless steps still tread the paths divine,
Though doubt withhold the light of hope benign.
With boundless yearning spurn the depths you 've
    trod,
And climb the dizzy heights where waits your God !''

The Prophet's eyes were lit with ardent light,
His earnest face, so thin, was marble white,
As one about to die, inspired to tell,
With voice of God, life's deathless miracle;
But Percival saw not the failing eye,
Enkindled as it was by ecstasy,—
Saw not the snowy brow, nor pallid cheek,
So thrilled he was, so eager still to seek
The truth that seemed to mock his vain desire,
In shadow vestments floating ever higher.

'' O tell me, Master, more of earth's domain,—
Albeit my quest seems futile and in vain,—
Of atoms shaped by law's resistless will
In forms innumerous, that haunt and fill
All space with wonder—by their chemic spell
Upbuilding life's unfathom'd miracle.''
So spoke the thoughtless youth. The Master said
In musing undertone, heart-wearièd:

THE PROMISE OF THE AGES.

" Reach upward, O world-soul, and span the domain
of the stars;
Gaze outward, and scan the unending contrivings of
time;
Peer inward, and view the swift atoms astir at thy
heart,—
The atoms all working together to further thy aims.
O world-soul, thy structure, so massive, is builded
entire
Of atoms that throng in a sun-mote, and throb in a
beam;
And the least thing is great in thy counting that
reckons the stars,
That numbers the sands of the sea-beach, the leaves
of the grove,
And the cells of the tissues, compacted with infinite
care.
What alchemy, passing all wonder, thy labor reveals,
As the atoms, each spelled to its duty, pass forth in
review,—
Combining and changing and ranging through worlds
and through time,—
Incessantly throbbing, and threading the mazes of
earth,—
Unerringly trained to the task they are doomed to
perform."

His words grew faint and died in sighs away,
And Percival beheld, with swift dismay,
The deadly weariness that shook his frame.
The youth's fair cheek was flushed with sudden shame
To think what weight of woe his thoughtless pride
Had caused to him his heart had deified.
The Prophet gently soothed his mind, contrite,
And laughed away his needless pang of fright;
Then, parting, promised many another walk,
And many an hour of sweet, regardful talk.

BOOK III.

O doubt that cannot be suppressed,
That twines its tendrils round the heart
And clings and grows forever there!
O love that waxeth strong with time,
That swells to fill the heart with bliss,
Till clogged by doubt, the parasite!
No note of time took Percival,
So deep engrossed his mind and heart,
While day slipped into night, and night,
Unheeded, lapsed again to day.
Oft-times he dreamed of sacrifice,—
Of losing self in him he loved,—
Of utter faith, unthinking, dead,—
The Prophet's word alone his law;
But, while he thought, a sense of shame
Crept like a vapor from the grave,
To shroud him in a sheet of scorn.
"Abandon self? Nay, not to God
Would I relinquish selfhood's claim!"
His spirit thrilled to own its right,—

29

To know itself a living soul.
Thus doubting, Percival beheld
The silent night that brooded round,
And spake these words amid the dark:

"Universe of solitude, where stars and atoms glide,
Desolate seclusion in the tempest-tossing time,
Ceaselessly evolving as the ages slowly ride
Onward toward accomplishment of purposes sublime,—
Ceaselessly upleading the potential to the light,
Tell me what the secret is thy heart has hid away;
Tell me what the spirit is that scans the hollow night,—
Tell me all the wonderment of life's unending day."

There is naught more fair than the heaving sea,
There is naught more strange than the boundless
    sky,
Save the mind that encompasseth sea and sky,
Save the love that enfoldeth the world in its spell.
And Percival rose from his dream of the night,
From his doubt and his pain, to a light, new grown,—
To the light from within that illumines the whole.

Full eagerly he sought the Prophet's side,
And they together walked beside the sea,—
There where the waters make perpetual moan.

THE PROMISE OF THE AGES.

The mad waves swept upon the sandy shore,
And, backward gliding, left strange tokens there,—
Frail lace-work wrought in green and gold and red,
Fit to adorn some mermaid's waving hair;
And shells of lustrous pearl the waves had filched
From caverns under sea, and creatures weird
That dwell amid the ever-silent deeps.
Here Percival addressed the sage, devout,
To ask from whence man's spirit wandered here,—
To learn what linked him to eternity.
Then mightily the Prophet's voice uprose,
(Mingling with ocean's massive undertone)
As there he stood, bareheaded, by the sea,
And answered thus the boy who worshiped him:

"This thundering epic of time and of tears,
With its terrible story, titanic and grim,
How it moves us to wonder and spells us with awe,
As we read it, and roam through its tumult and strife!
How awful this tale of the past with its troubles
Through conquering ages down-trampled by truth!
O time and eternity, battling unceasingly,
Never shall end this insatiate strife!

Am I but a spark, in the drama of ages,
That flashes from darkness and burns into naught,—

THE PROMISE OF THE AGES.

A bubble that floats on the ocean eternal,
And bursts on the crest of a white wave of time?
Nay, nay, I remember, in æons past counting,
When lowly I groped in the gloom of the sea,
In the glamourous gloom of the passionless deep,—
A lowly Ascidian, feeble and powerless,
Strong but in longing and yearning for light.

Silently, haltingly, ploddingly seeking,
I found the first treasure that heaven had sent,—
I found it and clung to its beauty and majesty,—
World without end it revealed to my sight !
The wonderful world of the sea and the silence
Were mine, only mine, to desire, to own;
I burst from my bondage with thoughts that aspired
Still higher amid the wide waste of the deep.
A fish I had grown, with the speed of the foam,
And I lashed through the waters and leaped at the
        stars;
I fled from the giants infesting the deep,
And I grew, ever grew, as the ages swept past.

I leaped at the stars, and I longed in my leaping
To breathe the free air of the crystalline sky;
Millenniums passed while I strove for my freedom,
And crept to the shore, there to grovel and toil,—

To crawl through the slime of the shores and the
    shallows,—
A reptilian thing I was destined to be,
Till the warmth and the passion, still latent within me,
Broke forth in my blood and impelled me to climb,—
To climb on the mountains,— to leap in the forest,—
To fight and to fall and to mount on the slain,—
To triumph exultant, with fangs deeply bedded
In the flesh of a foe, where the blood spurted
    fast,—
Relentlessly bedded, as, greedily gorging,
I fed on the foe I had conquered and killed.

All this I remember as backward I scan
The mighty world-epic that fate has unrolled,—
This epic of life I have lived in and longed in,
Have fought in and loved in through infinite time:
This past that has made me its slave and its master,
As, faster receding in wave after wave,
I stand and behold it, I clasp it,—infold it,
When lo! it retreats to its limitless grave!"

The Prophet ended thus, while Percival
Stood silent, filled with awe, and spoke no word;
But from the waves came voices deep and low,
Singing strange melodies in muffled tone,—

Wild runes from singers on some foreign strand,
The voice of prophecy from lips unseen:

Man regenerate,
Love insatiate,
Hope with joy elate,
Groping and growing,—
Thus our world shall be
Climbing to liberty,
Glad in its victory,
Reaping and sowing.

Not through faith alone,
Light on our journey shone;
Slowly our hope has grown,
Baffled while groping;
Sowing the seed we reap,
Strong from the tears we weep;
Love, that can never sleep,
Still keeps us hoping.

BOOK IV.

O mighty man with th' wistful eye,
Sad from th' untold troubles that made thee strong,
Hewn of the rock adversity, to stand,
A citadel where truth and love abide,
I dare not enter that celestial court,
Thy heart, to peer upon its hallowed sanctity.
No, rather let thy spirit, dove-like, brood
About the spring-time, bringing peace and rest,
Whilst thou, within thy fathomless abode,
Dost gaze forth calmly on th' awak'ning year,—
Gaze forth to see thy dearest hopes decline,—
Thy love return'd by cold forgetfulness.

The spring had come with glad, tumultuous song,
And ev'ry bird's young heart was keen with love.
The flowers came crowding through the sodden earth
And looked upon the glory of the sun.
Joy, joy and love were over all the land;
But Percival no longer walked abroad

With him who loved him day by day more dear,—
No longer thirsted for immortal truth,—
In moody solitude lone wandering.
The Master, with pleach'd arms and head downcast,
His long cloak folded round his fragile form,
Walk'd unattended 'mid the gladsome spring.
One time they met in haunts endeared of old,—
The youth, abashed, the Master, still the same,
Greeting his friend in unreproachful tone.

His gentleness o'ercame the boy's reserve,
And presently they talked, as when of old
They wandered gladly 'mid the wilderness.
But Percival no longer asked of stars,
Or atoms, or of life's unending toil,
Seeking in lieu their Fashioner divine,—
The God who worked these miracles of change.
The Prophet sadly answer'd him in tones
Of bitterness, like some deep song of death:

> *"On His mighty throne*
> *Sits the Great Unknown,*
> *Alone! alone!*
> *His throne is the world,*
> *And His voice is hurled*
> *Where the stars have flown.*

THE PROMISE OF THE AGES.

The skies are ringing
With mighty singing,
From the voice of the Great Unknown;
And I hear His song
In a world of wrong,
And bless each somber tone
Of the Great Unknown.
His song is the heart's deep moan
Of pity and love and longing,
In tumult thronging
From the world of the flesh — His throne!"

There was a sadness in the Master's voice,
A dread solemnity, that seemed to fall
Like organ tones from some cathedral pile,
Crumbling in hoar antiquity away;
And Percival drew near the Prophet's side,
And took his withered hand, and looked at him.
Something the youth would say, but knew not how.
Thus stood they, hand in hand, beneath the trees,
The spring's blest benediction over them,
Each for the other's unknown sorrow pain'd.

BOOK V.

There came a day, of all fair days most fair,
When birds, amid the budded boughs astir,
Were building, for their nestlings, downy homes,—
When ev'ry flow'r was sought by toiling bee
To bear its nectar to the hivèd cell;
But some strange trouble haunted Percival,
And spring's rare joyance only made him sad.
At last, disburdening his heavy heart,
The Prophet standing by to hear his pain,
He burst forth, praying to the pow'rs of time:

" O lift from my spirit this burden, this curse that I
    bear,
Like a felon in fetters, atoning for ages of sin.
The heir of eternity's sinning, I bend 'neath the load,
And wait for the crushing contention to lighten my
    pain,—
To drag me to darkness and chaos,—to scatter my
    breath

Like a plague and a pillage to people, a curse among
    men.
Heredity, awful usurper of time-growing souls,
Unpitying power appalling, that hearest no prayer,—
No prayer through the darkest desponding, no prayer
    from the heart,
O tell me why I should be chastened for sins of my
    sire;
Why, longing to grow, I am baffled, and sink to the
    earth,
To fester, forsaken, forgotten, by life's turbid throng,
While others surge upward, abetted by powers that
    guide
Th' inscrutable fate of the universe, time without
    mind!
Though stars grow and worlds grow, evolving to
    greater completeness,
Though life bears the tree of the ages to fruitage in
    man,
Though laws grow, and knowledge trends steadily
    upward and onward,
What counts this for me, thus accursed in the dark
    and defiled?"

Ah! there was pity in the Master's eye,
For Percival's drear plight and bitter plaint,

And tender speech he made consoling him:
" Nay, fate has not bequeathed so sad a load
To mar thy life with fell incertitude;
Thy father's curse may haunt thee like some ghost
Forever near,— perturbed and sick from sin, —
But thou art not thy father, nor the ghost
Of some ancestral wrong.   Be still thyself!
Forever shape thy way as God ordained,
And let no worldly fear encompass thee.
Not in a day, but in eternity,
The ghostly past is laid in some deep grave
Where sin falls dead and molds in dust away!"
" No, Master, not for self alone do I
Repine," said Percival, with anxious breath.
The other looked upon the ardent youth,
So pallidly beseeching him in pain,
And knew what mortal words could scarce convey.
" Then be of goodly cheer," the Master said,
And, turning, breathed a prayer of thankfulness,—
A prayer to Him who, deep in ev'ry heart
Lives and awaits fulfillment,—life for love:

"Lord, Thou hast toiled with this fair frame of mine
Through generations endless as the stars;
With ceaseless adaptation molding all
To fitness and fulfillment, perfect planned.

THE PROMISE OF THE AGES.

This eye, that glorifies my darkened soul
With light and beauty trembling from afar,
How hast Thou fashioned it with tireless toil!
When all was dim at life's umbrageous dawn,
Thy wisdom knew the wonder, unfulfilled,—
Transcendent miracle, by growth achieved!
This ear, that tells the soul of tones divine,
How didst Thou frame it when the world was young,—
In silence shaping then a sea of song,
Pent in the world's deep heart of mystery.
Yea, all the beauty, all the might of soul,
Has swum upon the flood of flowing time,
Breasting the currents of adversity!
O Lord, Thou hast ordained the laws of time
In all the wisdom of Thy perfect heart;
And I, who float upon its heaving breast,
With gratitude deep sunken in my soul,
Look back and wonder at its loveliness,—
Look back and see Thy godliness revealed
In law and harmony that live for aye,—
In love that cannot die, but deathless stands,
Flooding the world with light — a Holy Ghost
In ev'ry heart, that weaves all lives in one."

Tears were in Percival's fond eye,
And thankfulness upon his lip,

41

And joy was in his heart of hearts,
For that dread curse was lifted now,
By those sweet words of helpfulness,—
Those words of faith and trust and love;
And, as they homeward walked among
The dreaming trees, the Prophet told
Of love made manifest through endless toil,—
Of beauty woven into truth and trust:

A weaver is weaving away in seclusion,—
Is weaving a robe for immortals to wear;
I hear the low shuffle his shuttle is making,
In measures euphonic, in rhythmical time,—
The dulcet and canorous hum of his shuttle,
That weaves with unwavering, weariless faith.
The winds he is weaving — a warp for his fabric—
The winds of the dripping salt caves by the sea,—
The mellow meandering winds of the meadow,—
The forest winds, soughing and sobbing at night:
All these he is weaving, a warp for his fabric,—
All these, with the singing of birds and of men,—
The music of maidens, the laughing of children,
And lowing of cattle, as evening steals on.
The clouds and the sea are the woof for his weaving,—
The cumulus clouds as they climb through the sky,—
The pennants of sunset, all golden and crimson,—

THE PROMISE OF THE AGES.

The white waifs of summer that wander alone;
The sea, with its motion of turbulent waters,
Its crisp curling crests and its flurry of foam,—
Its blue waste of beauty, majestic and endless,—
Its boundless exuberance, battling for aye.
Thus weaving, with weariless music, his fabric,
The weaver unceasingly bends to his toil,—
He fashions a fabric of splendor supernal,
The gods to adorn in their peerless domain,—
A garment of glory to grace the immortals,—
A mantle of love for the children of heav'n.

BOOK VI.

There is a love which cometh with the spring,
   Unlike the gentle love of friend for friend,
A love which is not joy, nor anything
   But madness and desire that knows no end.
It cometh like the bird on bounding wing
   Amid the slumb'ring winter of the soul,
Its throat too full of melody, to sing
   The ardent rapture struggling for control.
Thus Percival had felt love's sweetest pain,
   And known its fiercest pang of fell despair,
Had lapsed into a dream where all was vain,
   Had wakened to a world where all was fair.
Above him swept the boundless waste of blue,
   Beneath him stretched the velvet fields of green,
Around him frailest flowers of spring-time grew,
   Beside him walked the maiden Merodine.

   Ah Merodine, dear Merodine,
     Large-eyed and tender hearted,

44

THE PROMISE OF THE AGES.

At thy name the birds all sang,
  And swift the flowers started
From their sleep to see thee pass,
  Merodine, dear Merodine!
What wonder, then, that Percival grew pale for love
  of thee!
What wonder that he gazed upon thy pure divinity
And felt a love that passeth earth's supreme felicity!

Percival and Merodine!
Two kindred creatures blent in one ideal,
Two spirits yearning for the one divine!
Now Percival, his heart aglow with love,
Taught his dear pupil from the Prophet's theme;
And she, more apt than he had been of old,
Drank, like a thirsting bird at life's cool spring,
The mystery and prophecy of love.
Upon a day of joy went Percival
With her he loved, to greet his cherished friend,
Who welcomed them full fondly, gazing long
At Merodine with tenderness and trust.
Her winning grace and earnest plaintive eye
He could not view insensibly, and she,
With adoration due, beheld the sage
As one illumined with a light divine.
It was a passing joy to Percival,

THE PROMISE OF THE AGES.

Such interchange of grace and love to find —
The fresh girl fancy tinged with vermeil glow
That warmed the hoary Prophet's pensive heart—
Until he felt steal o'er his life a pang
That tempered reason strove in vain to quell;
For Merodine was his, and he alone
Should treasure her heart-bounty, and should store
Each fond love-token from her trembling lip
In some sequested haunt by fancy wrought.
He shunned the Master now, and Merodine,
Whene'er she spoke of him, received reply
In words so cold they seemed reproving her.

Thus passed the spring, and thus the summer sped,
A wild love medley with the thrush sublime
To chant the vespers 'mid the solitude;
And autumn came and vanished like a dream,
Leaving stark winter, desolate and cold;
But, with the lapse of time, no word was said
Of him whose presence daily made them strong.
Only the gentle Merodine was sad
At thought of his drear solitude and pain.
For Percival was lost in love's abyss,
And heard no tone save Merodine's sweet voice,
And saw no shape save Merodine's dear form.
She knew not why such joy should come to her,

All undeserving, knew not why such bliss,
Intense to painfulness, was hers alone;
And sometimes, with her mild, enchanting eyes,
Beholding him, she looked within his soul
And trembled, overawed at such deep love,
And shuddered at the thought of losing him.

BOOK VII.

Happiness,—vain rapture of an hour,
Frail bubble that the prick of pain may burst
To nothingness, sweet strain that dies away
With th' last trembling chord that strikes the ear,
To live alone in memory's sad dream—
Thy fleeting spell is shattered into dust
As time's inexorable touch is laid
On that dear mansion of the deathless soul!

One morning, Merodine bespoke her love,
Her fair face pallid from a night of pain,
And said, with anxious look, and earnest tone:
" I dreamed of Death last night; I saw him stand
Beside a sea of sorrow. In his hand
A pale child dangled, with its waving hair
Tossed in the mournful, desecrating air
That would not be appeased. A mother's cry
Shuddered about his form unceasingly,
Until the moldering skulls that paved the earth

Shook, and looked up with grins of ghastly mirth;
While th' cobweb centuries, about them grown,
To nothingness were pitilessly blown.
The great black Death stood iron-like and stark,
His vacant eyes looked forth upon the dark,—
When O, thank God, I wakened from my dream,
And saw the pale moon through the window stream.
" Again I slept, and dreamed of Death anew,—
Of Death, the seraph fair, with eyes of blue,—
Of Death, the fond restorer, young and bright,
Leading the troubled soul to love and light,—
Beside still waters treading meadows green,
In that wide valley of the great unseen.
So lovely did he seem, that loud I cried,
O take me, Death, across that valley wide!"

It was a portent of dread circumstance,
This heavy-hearted dream that bade them stare
Upon the blackness of eternity
In wonder, and be dumb at death's stern call.
But Percival scorned all uncanny things,
And deigned not hearken to an idle dream,
Till Merodine recalled the Prophet, lone,
Unvisited, save by the wintry air
That knew no pity for his agéd head.
Then Percival was touched with sudden fear;

The old love surged across his life again —
The dear companionship, the ardent trust,
The cruel months of cold neglect and scorn,
The cruel months of selfish blissfulness!
"O Merodine, dear Merodine!" he cried,
"What strange enchantment thou didst breed in me,
To seal my eyes on thy dear orbs alone,
And with thy witchery to steal away
So utterly my ev'ry thought and dream!
Straightway I'll find him now, and fresh declare
The old faith stronger grown with lapse of time."
And Merodine said, "Go, and tell thy love
To him who pines for human fellowship."
He went, her mild eyes following in fear,
Her gentle love attending him afar.

BOOK VIII.

Well mayst thou step lightly, Percival,
　　And timidly, and fearfully, before
The Prophet's door, that echoed to thy knock
　　So loudly and so cheerfully of yore.
And well thy heart may palpitate with dread,
　　Thy heart that beat so bravely long ago,
And well thy lips may question, " Is he dead?"
　　And well thy mind may fear the truth to know!

He entered, and the Prophet lived,—O joy,
To make atonement now for past neglect,
To say all words of love in one long breath,—
To prove his pity and to hide his shame!
But some sad change the Master's bearing showed,
Some shock of time that left him doubly frail.
He looked with vacant eye at Percival,
Who trembled 'neath his strange unmeaning stare,
And could not tell the love oppressing him.
O dear old man, earth-weari'd, still enslaved

In life's frail shell, the spirit loth to flee,
Thou hast not toiled in vain! In ampler spheres
Thy soul shall seek fulfillment, earth-denied;
In vaster hearts thy love shall throb and grow
To infinite attainment, God-ordain'd!
But Percival, o'erwrought with pain and dread,
Sobb'd pitifully, " Master, canst not hear?
Have thy dear eyes forgot their cunning, too?"
The Prophet heard his speech and made return:
" Well, boy, and hast thou come to take me hence,
Down by the shore of the billowy sea
Where the waters lift their arms of snow
To beckon the wanderer on and on
O'er the sandy waste that reaches afar?
We have wandered oft together, boy, and oft
Beside the sea we dreamed our wondrous dream;
And now I cannot fear to go with thee
Along that endless shore we looked upon.
But first I have some words to say to thee,—
Some words I fain would speak so mightily
That all mankind their syllables would hear,
And all their meaning treasure unto death:

*"Man's love is the heart's love,— man's work and his
    lore
Is the spirit's assertion of freedom and life;*

THE PROMISE OF THE AGES.

Man's hope is the heart's hope,— man's faith and his
trust
Is the spirit's belief in the beauty of truth;
Man's truth is the soul's truth,— the soul's truth is
whole truth,
And the whole truth is God with His loving of Man.

Man's love is the Lord's love,— man's work and his
lore
Is the Lord's mighty planning, revealed in His sons;
Man's hope is the Lord's hope,—man's faith and his trust
Is the faith of the Lord in the beauty of truth;
Man's truth is the Lord's truth, that smites the heart's
chords' truth,
And the heart's chords are ringing with God's love
for man."

His eyes were burning with unnatural fire,
His limbs were tense with unconsum'd desire,
While Percival stood speechless and afraid,
Longing to help, yet stagger'd and dismay'd.
Then, on the impulse, swift as bird takes wing,
Towards Merodine the youth was hurrying;
And soon together speeded they in fear,
Bent to the lone abode of him so dear,
Who wandered deathwards in his lorn despair.

But death is not so fell a thing to thee,
O Prophet, for thy mighty heart can bear
All sorrows to oblivion, and see
Death shattered by the soul's immensity!
When Merodine and Percival drew nigh
Their best belovèd friend, so soon to die,
They could not weep, o'eraw'd by such sublime
Communion on the verge of parting time;
They could not speak, but only looked their pain —
Their eyes grown eloquent where words were vain.
At last the Prophet noticed them, and said,
"Who art thou? some dear spirits of the dead,
Sent to convey my weary soul afar,
Sky-dwellers wander'd from thy lucent star?"
"Nay, Master," Percival replied; "thy end
Is not so near. Thy way shall trend
Still on amid life's labyrinth of good,
Thy soul denied death's somber sisterhood."

New strength infused the Prophet's sinking frame,
As thus uprose his last supreme proclaim:
" There is no death, for the soul must measure the
    soul;
And the world is a dream, and the wold that we deem
The end of the soul, like the clouds that roll,
Will melt from the light into mist of the night,

And sing in its flight of the beautiful whole.
There is no death,—and the grave, like the wave,
Sweeps over our heads, till we sink in its bed,
To rise with the dead, from our turbulent cave.

" The world is a dream, and its white ghosts teem
In the tottering brain; but we seek in vain
For the host of the dead, who are fled! fled! fled!
They have fled into life, they have burst from the
    strife
Of the world of to-day, with its doubt and dismay,—
And their fleet steps wend toward the limitless end,
With its infinite gain they may never attain;
But the rapture of striving and growing will blend
With the longings that ever with love will contend,
As they see through the tears of eternity, far,
God's love, like the light of His passionate star."

Thus ending, Merodine bent over him,
And kissed his brow, and wept, while Percival
Enclasped his hand — his heart too full for words.
Then, with a passing sigh, the Master's soul
Slipped from the dull entanglement of earth,
In ampler spheres to labor up to God.
Weep, earth children, weep for him who loved
Both thee and all thy people far and wide;

THE PROMISE OF THE AGES.

For he has gone from thee and left thee lone !
But O rejoice to know thy heritage
Which time cannot efface, nor change can mar!
Here, in the awful presence of the dead,
Rejoice in that great heritage of love.
For, out of death, the soul, reborn, shall wing
Its way in glory 'mid a fairer spring,
And, out of doubt and pain, shall rise to be
Love's emblem, bearing hope and immortality,
Singing afar in God's grand hierarchy:

Spirits of beauty, in glory attired,
I call thee and claim thee, by heaven inspired!
Together we'll float through the azure sublime
On pinions of love, where the turmoil of time
Is lost in the infinite glory of light,
Transcending the lowly, uplifting the right;
Together we'll sing with the spheres that are chanting
A love that o'erreaches our passionate panting;
Together we'll triumph o'er trouble and pain,
Recalled from earth's toil to an ampler domain;
And God shall await us, completing His plan
When the conquering angel has wrestled with man.